Lessons in Chemistry

By Jaxon Savige

"Lessons in Chemistry" is an enthralling exploration of the life and career of Dr. Elizabeth Harper, a brilliant chemist whose journey unfolds against the backdrop of the picturesque town of Brooksville. As a woman navigating the complex world of academia, Elizabeth faces formidable challenges and societal expectations, breaking through the glass ceiling with tenacity and brilliance.

The narrative delves into Elizabeth's early fascination with chemistry, her struggles against gender bias, and the mentorship experiences that shape her trajectory. The story takes an unexpected turn when she encounters Emily, a troubled high school student, and discovers the transformative power of mentorship, not only in the realm of science but in the broader tapestry of life.

As Elizabeth rises through the ranks in academia, readers witness her grappling with ethical dilemmas, forming meaningful connections, and navigating the intricate chemistry of personal relationships. The book explores themes of resilience, determination, and the delicate balance between professional success and personal fulfillment.

"Lessons in Chemistry" is a journey through the periodic table of life, where each chapter represents an element in Elizabeth's story. From the dynamics of leadership to the alchemy of teaching, the book weaves together the scientific and personal dimensions of her life, culminating in a legacy that extends beyond the laboratory.

The narrative is rich with insights into the world of science, touching on the importance of mentorship, the challenges faced by women in STEM, and the ethical considerations inherent in scientific discovery. Ultimately, "Lessons in Chemistry" is a celebration of the indomitable spirit that propels individuals to challenge boundaries, redefine success, and leave an enduring mark on the scientific landscape.

CONTENTS

Chapter 1:

The Brooksville Chronicles

The village was trapped in a time warp right in the middle of Brooksville, where the vast apple orchards and the undulating hills met. The smell of flowering flowers drifted into the air like a song, and each cobblestone street reverberated with the whispers of tradition. This quaint community, complete with antique buildings and white picket fences, served as more than just a setting for Dr. Elizabeth Harper's story.

Brooksville woke up to the promise of a new day as the sun rose and painted the sky in shades of pink and gold. The residents of the settlement, a close-knit group united by kinship and common experiences, started their everyday lives. Warm greetings were given and received, and the streets were lined with familiar faces that carried memories from bygone eras.

The Brooksville Chronicles began among the ageless beauty of the town; they are a real, breathing record of the ups and downs of life in this idyllic refuge. Brooksville was a monument to the enduring power of tradition, from the busy town square, where the smells of freshly made apple pies filled the air, to the peaceful lanes dotted with centuries-old oak trees.

Dr. Elizabeth Harper found her niche at Brooksville University, where academic pursuits and knowledge-seeking collide. Her entrance into the community was a seismic event, one that would upend the balance of accepted conventions. As the town and its newest member got to know one another, the story that would become woven into Brooksville's very fabric started to take shape.

Readers would see the dance between tradition and progress, community and individualism, as the Brooksville Chronicles developed. Elizabeth would paint her imprint on the town's vitality and character, and Brooksville would leave an enduring impression on the lady who dared to question the current quo.

In "The Brooksville Chronicles," the town transforms from a backdrop into a living, breathing organism that both shapes and is shaped by the people who live there. The chapter invites readers to set off on a journey that beyond the confines of time and tradition by laying the groundwork for the interwoven fates of Elizabeth Harper and Brooksville.

Chapter 2:

Chemical Origins

In Elizabeth Harper's early years, her curiosity acted as a trigger for a series of scientific investigations in the laboratory. She showed an early passion with the realm of atoms and molecules, as well as an almost insatiable curiosity. Her initial explorations into the mysteries of chemistry took place in her father's improvised home laboratory.

It was among the seething mixtures and glass beakers that Elizabeth found the alchemy of metamorphosis. Her tests involved common household objects, and each reaction—whether fizzing or foaming—felt like a tiny epiphany. Her eighth birthday present from her parents was a chemical kit that opened a realm where mysteries of the cosmos were hidden in the seemingly ordinary.

As she advanced in her education, the periodic table served as a road map that helped her navigate the challenging terrain of elements. Her scholastic career was accompanied by the hum of fluorescent lights and the fragrance of textbooks. Elizabeth started to understand the deep beauty of the molecular dance that ruled the natural world in classrooms and libraries.

However, it involved more than simply mathematics and formulae. Elizabeth saw chemistry as a language, a way to interpret the poetry encoded in the forms of matter. With its well-organized rows and columns, the periodic table evolved into a literary masterpiece, with each element narrating a distinct story of bonds, electrons, and reactions.

Elizabeth ran across naysayers in her search for knowledge, those who doubted a small child's suitability for the world of test tubes and Bunsen burners. Nevertheless, her enthusiasm for the topic was greater than any blaze in the lab. She demonstrated that chemistry is a love that knows no bounds to age or gender by overcoming each obstacle with the tenacity of a genuine scientist.

The chapter "Chemical Beginnings" describes Elizabeth's early years of her scientific career. It's a story laced with the magic of childhood, parental support, and the excitement of exploration. Readers are allowed to witness the birth of a bright mind that would go on to have a lasting impact on the field of science when Elizabeth ventures into the field of chemistry for the first time.

Chapter 3:

The Glass Ceiling

Even with the regalia of knowledge, the academic halls were not immune to the ubiquitous limitations of society expectations. Elizabeth Harper realized as she moved up the academic ladder that there was an immovable but tangible barrier—the so-called "glass ceiling"—in her path.

Gender prejudice was a pervasive albeit subtle force in the lecture halls and laboratories. Unconsciously, colleagues frequently questioned whether a woman could spearhead innovative research or demand the same level of respect as their male counterparts. Elizabeth's goals were shadowed by the imposing glass ceiling.

Elizabeth was unfazed and saw the glass ceiling as a challenge to be overcome rather than a barrier. Equipped with an ingenious intellect and an unwavering resolve, she persevered, questioning preconceived assumptions at every opportunity. Once an inspiration, the periodic table turned into a symbolic battlefield where she battled for acceptance and respect.

Still, the glass ceiling was not unique to the laboratory. It was present in every aspect of Elizabeth's life, including informal chats and business gatherings. She discovered that, as a woman in science, she had to balance both negotiating the delicate nuances of society expectations and demonstrating her knowledge. Nevertheless, she eroded the glass with each scientific discovery, creating cracks in the formerly impenetrable surface.

In this uphill battle, allies and mentors proved invaluable. Elizabeth learned the strength that comes from unity as she overcame hardship. Her support was bolstered by the solidarity of female coworkers and proponents of gender parity, who saw the glass ceiling as a fault that could be overcome with group endeavor rather than an impassable obstacle.

A chapter titled "The Glass Ceiling" explores the subtleties of gender dynamics in the scientific community. It gives a clear picture of Elizabeth's journey as she faces prejudices, dispels myths, and works to go beyond the boundaries set by society norms. Elizabeth Harper overcomes hardship to become not just a brilliant scientist but also a trailblazer who breaks down the glass ceiling for future generations.

Chapter 4:

The Value of Mentoring

Elizabeth Harper found a mooring amid the tumultuous waters of academia: the transforming potential of mentorship. She was fortunate to have mentors who guided her through the often tumultuous waters of her career, helping to shape not just her scientific ability but also her fortitude in the face of adversity.

Dr. Eleanor Mitchell, the first mentor, was a renowned expert in the field of chemistry. Dr. Mitchell, who exuded a calmness akin to the elements she researched, saw Elizabeth's potential even in her early academic career. Elizabeth refined her abilities under her tutelage, mastering not just the complexities of chemical reactions but also the art of negotiating the academic environment as a female scientist.

The advice of Dr. Mitchell was not limited to the lab. She gave priceless leadership lessons, stressing the need of tenacity and perseverance in the quest of scientific greatness. Equipped with the understanding that her abilities had no bounds by gender, Elizabeth started to see the glass ceiling as a surface to break through rather than an obstacle thanks to her mentor's consistent support.

Professor Samuel Rodriguez became Elizabeth's second professional mentor as she advanced in her career. Professor Rodriguez became an advocate for diversity in STEM after pioneering the process of tearing down barriers for marginalized minorities. His guidance extended beyond the classroom, teaching Elizabeth that promoting an inclusive and egalitarian atmosphere was essential to achieving scientific greatness.

The dynamic of mentoring turned into a two-way street. Elizabeth became a mentor herself as she internalized the knowledge that her mentors imparted to her. As she developed the abilities of younger scientists, she realized how important it was to return the favor of mentoring, causing a chain reaction of empowerment among scientists.

The chapter "Mentorship Matters" delves into the significant influence that mentoring had on Elizabeth Harper's life path. It draws attention to the critical role mentors played in molding her personality, fostering resiliency, and igniting her quest for excellence in science. The chapter emphasizes the value of creating a community of support that spans generations and leaves a legacy of inspiration and direction via the perspective of mentorship.

Chapter 5:

Severing Connections

There were difficult times along Dr. Elizabeth Harper's path from bright young scientist to ground-breaking investigator. Throughout her career, she faced opposition, doubt, and unwavering pressure to fit in with society's expectations. "Breaking Bonds" honors Elizabeth's victories over misfortune and documents her journey through these difficulties.

Elizabeth encountered doubts from colleagues who questioned the validity of her scientific contributions as she dug deeper into her studies. Elizabeth's unwavering love for chemistry drove her to overcome the limitations imposed by traditional gender stereotypes that tried to keep her in specific areas. Her achievements in the lab served as evidence of the fallacy of trying to stifle genius within the restrictive confines of gender norms.

The more Elizabeth's notoriety, the more pressure there was from society to fit in. The media tried to fit her story into preconceived notions because of its ravenous need for stories. Elizabeth, however, remained unwavering in her defiance of the restrictive stereotypes that attempted to define her. She embraced her identity as a scientist without apology, severing the shackles of social expectations.

In the scholarly sphere, where power structures frequently determined outcomes, Elizabeth had to pave her own way. She defied the conventions that tried to keep her on the fringes, but she handled the maze of higher education with poise and resolve. Working together with like-minded people helped to tear down barriers and transform the environment for upcoming scientists.

"Breaking Bonds" is a chapter on tenacity, bravery, and pursuing one's passion unwaveringly. It reveals the social and professional limitations Elizabeth faced and presents her as a catalyst for transformation. Elizabeth Harper proves herself as a role model for people who dare to question the current quo by overcoming obstacles and shining a light on the idea that talent has no bounds.

Chapter 6:

The Change-Catalyst

Sometimes, in the laboratory of life, random meetings are the triggers that set off significant changes. This moment for Dr. Elizabeth Harper arrived in the form of Emily, a problematic high school student. Elizabeth learned that mentoring might be a powerful driver for resilience and personal development in addition to academic success as fate intertwined their paths.

Emily turned out to be an unexpected apprentice, with a troubled past and a passion for chemistry that reflected Elizabeth's own young ardor. The mentorship that developed took place outside of beakers and textbooks. Elizabeth became into more than simply a chemistry teacher; she also became a ray of hope for a young person struggling to understand the intricacies of life.

As Elizabeth and Emily worked side by side on research, the lab turned into a safe haven where life lessons and academic knowledge blended together. The periodic table, which was formerly a strict arrangement of elements, changed into a blueprint of opportunities that helped Emily navigate the difficult turns on the journey toward self-discovery.

The relationship between the mentor and mentee was symbiotic, resulting in a product that was more powerful than the sum of its parts. Emily took strength from Emily's leadership, while Elizabeth was inspired by Emily's tenacity. They overcame obstacles together as they negotiated the difficulties of academia, believing that a strong desire and unwavering determination could conquer any hurdle.

"The Catalyst of Change" examines the transformational potential of mentoring, demonstrating how a single connection may change the direction of scientific research as well as the life of an individual. Elizabeth discovered via Emily that the influence of mentoring goes well beyond the confines of the lab and into the very fabric of society, where people who have the courage to believe in the potential of others sow the seeds of change.

Chapter 7:

Affiliates and Collaborators

Scientific pursuits are frequently shaped by alliances and cooperation in the complex dance of academia. "Lab Partners and Alliances" presents a period in the career of Dr. Elizabeth Harper in which she establishes ties outside of the laboratory by navigating the complex web of professional relationships.

Elizabeth's ascent to scientific renown was not an isolated path; rather, it was entwined with her colleagues' cooperative energies. She saw more and more how important it was to form alliances as she advanced through the academic ranks. Similar to the relationships she studied in her research, the chemistry among coworkers has the potential to be transformational.

Through collaborations, many viewpoints were brought together to create a synergy that advanced scientific investigation to unprecedented levels. Elizabeth found the strength of group intelligence in shared labs and cooperative initiatives. Lab partners developed into comrades in the quest of knowledge, pushing and encouraging one another to explore uncharted territory. They went beyond simple coworkers.

The voyage was not without difficulties, though. The complexities of chemical processes were reflected in the subtleties of professional interactions. Academic competition, competing personalities, and divergent approaches created obstacles that required a careful balancing act between diplomacy and resolve.

"Lab Partners and Alliances" explores the highs and lows of interpersonal conflicts as it digs into the complex dynamics of teamwork. Elizabeth discovered via her experiences with highs and lows that the relationships developed in the lab were essential to the advancement of science as well as the intellectual and emotional well-being of the scientific community.

This chapter presents Elizabeth Harper as a scientist who recognizes that academic partnerships are significant sources of inspiration, support, and intellectual development in addition to being tactically essential. Her scientific achievements are driven by her collaborative mentality, demonstrating that knowledge acquisition is fundamentally a group and collaborative undertaking.

Chapter 8:

Morality in Scientific Research

The ethical issues surrounding testing serve as a vital compass in the field of scientific inquiry, where the frontiers of knowledge are constantly being pushed. As a key chapter in Dr. Elizabeth Harper's story, "Ethics in Experimentation" delves into the complex moral terrain that surrounds the search for novel insights.

Elizabeth discovered herself at the nexus of creativity

and accountability as she dug further into her studies. Her conscience was troubled by the possible fallout from her research. Once a list of options, the periodic table now presented moral conundrums that required serious thought.

As the chapter progresses, Elizabeth finds herself considering issues that go beyond the lab's uncontaminated walls. What effects do her findings have on society? What possible effects might her findings have on ecosystems, communities, or even global dynamics? These were moral conundrums as much as scientific ones, requiring a careful balancing act between advancement and moral obligation.

There are pressures from both the inside and the outside as the story progresses. Elizabeth must walk a tightrope between scientific advancement and the possible harm it can do while coming under fire from organizations and peers. This chapter examines the morally difficult decisions that arise while making ethical decisions, showing that knowledge acquisition is not without its challenges.

"Ethics in Experimentation" explores Elizabeth's decisions about these moral conundrums. It illuminates the costs, the restless evenings, and the internal arguments that come with the duty of being a scientist. Through this investigation, the chapter hopes to raise more general concerns with the readers regarding the moral obligations of scientific research and the fine line that separates advancement from the possible drawbacks of going beyond what is now understood.

Chapter 9:

Leadership Dynamics

In the dynamic world of academia, leadership is more than just a title; it is a force that actively directs the course of scientific research. "The Dynamics of Leadership" opens a new chapter in the life of Dr. Elizabeth Harper, one in which she moves up the ranks and learns to navigate the challenges of leadership while having a clear awareness of the responsibilities that come with it.

Elizabeth's career's periodic table gradually changes as she takes on leadership jobs. Once reactive and experimental, mentoring and cooperation now come together under the heading of leadership to produce a synthesis of direction and creativity. The laboratory is not merely the physical space where tests are conducted, but also the individuals that work there.

The chapter delves into the struggles and achievements of academic leadership, which involves balancing directing research priorities with fostering the development of subordinates. Elizabeth is in charge, making choices that affect the direction of her organization, department, and, consequently, the scientific community as a whole.

Elizabeth is also introduced to the complex interactions of personalities in the academic ecosystem through the dynamics of leadership. As she negotiates the politics of cooperation and rivalry, she discovers that true leadership is creating an atmosphere where a variety of skills can flourish and add to the story of science as a whole. True leadership transcends individual success.

"The Dynamics of Leadership" provides readers with an understanding of Elizabeth's changing leadership role. In her quest to establish an environment that fosters scientific inquiry, it examines the conflict between creativity and stability, aspiration and empathy. The chapter poses questions on what it means to be a leader in the scientific community and the careful balancing act needed to mentor and inspire the following generation of scientists.

Chapter 10:

Lab-Based Learning

At the pinnacle of Dr. Elizabeth Harper's career, the lab evolves from a place for scientific research into a furnace that imparts priceless life lessons. "Lessons from the Lab" develops as a chapter in which Elizabeth considers the deep realizations attained from years of trial and error, failures, and ground-breaking findings.

Elizabeth learns the art of resilience in the controlled

turmoil of the lab. Experiments that fail ser
learning opportunity and a roadblock to f'
discoveries. Every unanticipated outcome ⸜.
departure from the norm serves as a teaching tou.
flexibility and the value of accepting the unknown.

Once a systematic framework, the periodic table
transforms into a metaphor for the unpredictable nature
of science and life. Elizabeth muses over the similarities
between the rhythm of life and the ebb and flow of
chemical reactions. It dawns on you that people and
situations are always changing, much like the
components of a reaction.

The chapter explores the relationship between discipline
and passion. Elizabeth muses about the times of
scientific euphoria when a hypothesis comes true as
well as the perseverance needed to get through the
tiresome and unreliable stages of study. It turns into a
contemplation on how to strike a balance between the
excitement of discovery and the perseverance needed
for scientific research.

Elizabeth shares knowledge learned from the
laboratory's crucible through the story. These are not
only scientific facts; they are also valuable life lessons
about perseverance, humility, and the intricate
connections among all human experiences. The chapter
poses questions for readers to consider, such as the
universal truths that underlie knowledge acquisition and
the laboratory's use as a metaphor for the larger
process of self-discovery.

he chapter "Lessons from the Lab" connects the scientific and human aspects of Dr. Elizabeth Harper's story and captures the spirit of her journey. It is a contemplation of the priceless knowledge acquired from the lab, where each experiment turns into a miniature version of life's lessons that are just waiting to be figured out.

Chapter 11:

The Friendship Chemistry

The chemistry of friendship is the harmonizing music that plays in Dr. Elizabeth Harper's life's symphony. This chapter explores the deep relationships she makes outside of the lab—ties that stand the test of time, hardships, and victories.

Elizabeth finds comfort and strength in the companionship of like-minded people as she makes her way through the challenging currents of academics. Coworkers develop become confidantes, and enduring friendships are rooted in a passion for research. The lab bench becomes a forum for ideas, humor, and mutual celebration of successes and turning points in addition to being used for research.

Originally intended to serve as a foundation for comprehending the elements, Elizabeth's world's varied personalities are symbolized by the periodic table.

Every buddy adds something special to the colorful fabric of her life. The dynamic exchanges, mutual benefits, and sporadic reactions that define the chemistry of genuine friendship are examined in this chapter.

Elizabeth learns that friendship is a combination of shared experiences and empathy. Her pals turn become sounding boards, pillars of support, and vital sources of counsel as she encounters obstacles in both her personal and professional lives. The stability of true friendship emerges from its consistency in the flux of life's responses.

"The Chemistry of Friendship" takes readers into the private world of Elizabeth's relationships with others, going beyond the confines of scientific inquiry. It is a celebration of the deep influence friendship can have on a person's journey and a reminder that, just like in the lab, teams of people working together to achieve a common goal frequently produce the most amazing discoveries.

Readers are able to observe the power of friendship as a defining factor in Elizabeth's life, helping to mold her personality and determine the course of her incredible adventure. The chapter turns into a monument to the transforming force of human relationships, showing how important friendships are even in the quest for scientific brilliance.

Chapter 12:

Compounds and Love

The chapter "Love and Compounds" delves into the intricacies of Dr. Elizabeth Harper's life, offering a sophisticated examination of the pleasures and complexities entwined in her intimate bonds. In the midst of scholarly and scientific activities, love shows up as a transformational force that challenges preconceptions and gives her story more depth.

Elizabeth becomes enmeshed in the delicate links of romantic relationships as her journey progresses. Originally intended to serve as a guide through the complexities of elements, the periodic table has come to represent the many elements that make up the chemistry of love, including trust, communication, passion, and the constant possibility of a response.

The chapter explores how love can be both beautifully transformational and unpredictable, like to a chemical reaction, as it navigates the ups and downs of romantic relationships. Elizabeth struggles to strike a balance between her personal and professional goals and learns that love is a complementing force that fosters her creativity and perseverance rather than a diversion from her scientific aspirations.

Elizabeth shares intimate moments with the reader via the story, including quiet discussions, times of laughter, and the kind support of a partner who is aware of the complexities of her scientific endeavors. Once a lonely place of study, the laboratory is now a social area where trials of life and love are conducted.

The chapter "Love and Compounds" illustrates how Elizabeth's personal and professional lives are intertwined and goes beyond traditional boundaries. It explores the transformational potential of love and shows how, like in science, the most meaningful discoveries can result from the complex interactions between different parts.

In the same way that the periodic table provides a framework for comprehending the characteristics of elements, "Love and Compounds" sheds light on the crucial role that love played in determining Elizabeth Harper's life's course and presents a complete picture of the complex woman who lived behind the scientist.

Chapter 13:

Impacts and Responses

"Collisions and Reactions" is a chapter that delves into the unexpected crossovers between personal and professional domains in the life story of Dr. Elizabeth Harper. Elizabeth struggles with the clashes of opposing aspects as her trip develops: ambition and contentment, job and life, passion and pragmatism.

Elizabeth is negotiating the complex interactions

between various components in the controlled and unplanned laboratory of existence. Her priorities shift in a way that completely changes the face of her identity as her aspirations for her career clash with her need for personal fulfillment.

The chapter explores critical times where opposing forces collide and produce unexpected outcomes. It's a story of self-discovery as Elizabeth wrestles with the difficult decisions that come up when her personal and professional lives intersect. Aspirations and reality colliding creates a furnace for development and change.

Elizabeth discovers how to negotiate the clashes between her own goals, those of society, and the unpredictability of interpersonal interactions while using the periodic table as a guide in the lab. This chapter emphasizes the intricacy of a life well lived, one in which accidents serve as catalysts for evolution rather than just as disturbances.

The book "Collisions and Reactions" asks readers to consider the fine line that separates following one's passions from accepting the unanticipated outcomes of life's collisions. It is evidence of the tenacity and flexibility needed to prosper in the face of constantly changing circumstances in both personal and professional life. Elizabeth's journey becomes a general investigation of the fine balance between aim and happenstance through the story.

Chapter 14:

Time as a Solvent

"The Solvent of Time" is a meditative chapter that delves into the significant impact of time passing on Dr. Elizabeth Harper's journey within the intricate tapestry of her life. Elizabeth's work and identity are shaped by the passage of time, which exhibits both transformational and erosive effects as the years pass.

The chapter explores Elizabeth's introspective moments as she struggles with time's unrelenting passage. Originally a static reference, the periodic table now serves as a metaphor for her life's changing phases. Every component, serving as a symbol for various chapters, has unique reactions and changes as the passage of time dissolves and reshapes the connections between experiences.

The passage of time presents Elizabeth with both an opportunity and a struggle as she navigates the shifting terrains of her personal and professional lives. It breaks certain preconceived notions and exposes previously undiscovered sides of her personality, but it also acts as a conduit for the blending of experience, resiliency, and life lessons.

The chapter skillfully crafts a story that spans several decades, encapsulating the key events that shape Elizabeth's legacy. It considers how things always change and how wisdom is acquired through the passage of time—how past struggles turn into lessons learned and triumphs into enduring accomplishments.

"The Solvent of Time" challenges readers to consider how the human experience is universal as it develops across time. It's a reflection on the nature of change— that which is inevitable—the flexibility needed to deal with life's reactions, and the way identity changes throughout time due to the passage of time. Readers can examine their own relationship with the ever-evolving, ever-flowing river of time by using Elizabeth's journey as a prism.

Chapter 15:

Teaching Alchemy

"Alchemy of Teaching" opens as a chapter that sheds light on the transformational power of education just as Dr. Elizabeth Harper approaches the stage in her career where experience and knowledge collide. Elizabeth learns about the alchemical process in the classroom that turns information into inspiration and makes students the agents of a lasting legacy.

Elizabeth's classroom is filled with various brains, and the periodic table, which formerly served as a guide through the elements of science, now becomes a metaphor for them. Every student is a distinct component with the capacity to elicit responses outside of the classroom. She learns that the alchemy of teaching involves more than just dispensing knowledge—it also entails sparking a shift in perspective and way of thinking.

The chapter explores Elizabeth's function as an instructor and mentor. Her successful and difficult experiences serve as the furnace in which the qualities of enthusiasm, curiosity, and resiliency come together to produce a life-changing learning opportunity. The classroom turns into an intellectual laboratory, and instruction takes on the form of a careful balancing act between structure and intuition.

Elizabeth observes the alchemical processes of comprehension and illumination as she walks her students through the complexities of chemistry. Mentor-mentee relationships develop into symbiotic partnerships in which the teacher and the mentee experience transformations that go beyond the classroom.

"Alchemy of Teaching" honors educators who, like Elizabeth, traverse the ever-changing academic terrain with a dedication to molding the minds of future generations. It asks readers to consider the long-lasting effects of inspirational educators and the significant impact that learning can have on the alchemical processes involved in self-discovery.

Through the alchemy of teaching, Dr. Elizabeth Harper leaves an enduring legacy on the scientific community that goes beyond her pioneering research and gets ingrained in the minds of those she instructs.

Chapter 16:

Empowerment's Components

"The Elements of Empowerment" is a chapter that delves into Dr. Elizabeth Harper's dedication to empowering people, especially women, in the traditionally male-dominated field of science. It appears in the chronicles of her life. This chapter explores the steps she takes and the activities she takes to make the scientific community a more equal and inclusive place.

Elizabeth understands the importance of diversity because the periodic table represents the variety of elements that make up the scientific community. Her ceaseless attempts to dismantle obstacles and give voice to others who, like herself, might encounter hardship because of their gender or other circumstances are demonstrated throughout the chapter. Once serving as a guide for chemical elements, the periodic table is now used as a model for promoting equality and diversity.

Elizabeth's path of self-determination goes beyond the classroom and lab. She turns becomes a champion of structural adjustment, opposing establishments and customs that uphold injustice. The chapter demonstrates how individual tales add to the larger story of progress by examining the dynamic interaction between the purpose of empowerment and personal experience.

Elizabeth wants to change science by becoming a more inclusive and approachable field through leadership, activism, and mentoring. The periodic chart, which shows the elements and how they interact, comes to symbolize the teamwork needed to bring about long-lasting change.

"The Elements of Empowerment" challenges readers to consider the larger effects of diversity in science and the value of giving marginalized perspectives a forum. Elizabeth's tale serves as a springboard for discussions on diversity and the complex concept of empowerment, reiterating the idea that genuine scientific advancement necessitates the active involvement of a wide range of viewpoints and thoughts.

Chapter 17:

Going Beyond the Lab Coat

"Beyond the Lab Coat" shows up as a chapter that goes beyond the boundaries of Dr. Elizabeth Harper's professional identity as her journey develops, providing a window into the many facets of her existence. This chapter takes off the scientist's lab coat to uncover the real human, complete with vulnerabilities, passions, and the rich tapestry of a life well lived.

Once a scholarly reference, the periodic table now serves as a mirror reflecting Elizabeth's complex individuality. This chapter presents a picture of the woman who, in addition to her innovative studies and mentoring, is influenced by a wide range of extracurricular activities, interpersonal connections, and life experiences.

Elizabeth invites readers to share in her happy and fulfilling private moments, interests, and personal endeavors. "Beyond the Lab Coat" examines the variety of experiences that make up a rich and meaningful existence, whether it's the comfort that comes from being in nature, the excitement of creating art, or the small joys of daily living.

This chapter explores Elizabeth's dealings with the world outside of academia, including her relationships with her community, the social implications of her work, and the ways in which she juggles her dual identities as a scientist and a human being. It is an honoring of the peaceful cohabitation of scientific passion with the various components of a well-rounded life.

"Beyond the Lab Coat" questions the conventional notion of a scientist as someone who is only defined by their professional endeavors and encourages readers to think about the holistic aspect of a fulfilled living. Elizabeth's narrative serves as an example of the delicate balancing act between ambition and contentment, life and work, and the eternal truth that, underneath the lab coat, there is a person with a wonderfully deep and diverse identity.

Chapter 18:

Parenting in Science

"Scientific Parenthood" develops as a chapter that examines the delicate balance between a successful career in science and the pleasures and difficulties of parenthood in Dr. Elizabeth Harper's story continuum. This chapter explores the relationship between a person's passion for their work and the significant obligations and changes that come with being a parent.

The complex chemistry of family life is metaphorically represented by the periodic table, which stands for the elements that make up the scientific realm. Striking a balance between the regimented world of research and the uncertain terrain of childrearing, Elizabeth finds herself conducting experiments of a new kind as she navigates the spheres of academia and parenthood.

The chapter begins with the rewards and challenges of being a scientist's parent. Elizabeth's journey serves as a testament to the dynamic interplay between the roles of scientist and parent, from the sleepless nights that come with a newborn's arrival to the rewarding moments of seeing a child's curiosity blossom.

Once a tool for comprehending the characteristics of

elements, the periodic table now serves as a roadmap for navigating the nuanced feelings and decisions that come with being a parent. This chapter encourages readers to reflect on the common experiences of juggling one's personal and professional identities, as well as the benefits and drawbacks of being a scientific parent.

"Scientific Parenthood" examines the ways in which raising a family and pursuing science inform and enhance one another. It's a celebration of the distinct insights and resiliency that come from this complex dance, as well as an acknowledgement of the difficulties experienced by those who aim to succeed in both fields.

Readers are encouraged to consider the larger issue of work-life integration by means of Elizabeth's story, realizing that, akin to elements on the periodic table, the various aspects of life can coexist in a harmonious and nourishing way.

Chapter 19:

Signs of the Moon and Stars

"Eclipses and Epiphanies" appears as a chapter that explores moments of tremendous revelation, both heavenly and personal, in the unfolding story of Dr. Elizabeth Harper's life. Elizabeth uses the concept of eclipses as a lens to see the light and shadows and uncover new facets of both the outside world and herself.

Emblematic of the ordered sequence of elements, the periodic table becomes a canvas for the eclipses that throw shadows over Elizabeth's scientific and psychological journey. As the chapter progresses, heavenly occurrences reflect life's ups and downs, inspiring reflection and igniting insights that direct her course.

The story looks at Elizabeth's eclipse moments in her scientific endeavors—moments when obstacles made it difficult for her to see clearly, but then she came across insights that helped her move forward. It reflects the cyclical nature of scientific research, in which periods of ambiguity and darkness frequently precede important breakthroughs.

In this chapter, personal eclipses also take major stage. Elizabeth struggles with the inequalities of life, including self-doubt, bereavement, and the shadows that always follow even the most promising of journeys. Through these personal eclipses, she learns resiliency, acquires fresh viewpoints, and has life-changing realizations that completely reshape her conception of who she is and what she wants to accomplish.

"Eclipses and Epiphanies" asks readers to consider how these heavenly occurrences are dual, comparing them to the highs and lows that are a part of life. It serves as a reminder that life is a dynamic interplay of elements— of shade and light, struggles and victories—much like the periodic table.

Readers are encouraged to consider their own eclipses and epiphanies as a result of Elizabeth's journey, realizing that these periods of darkness and light add to the rich fabric of a purposeful and contemplative existence.

Chapter 20:

The Quantum Transition

The chapter "The Quantum Leap" unfolds as Dr. Elizabeth Harper's story reaches its peak, capturing a critical period of significant advancement and change. This chapter examines a turning point in Elizabeth's career when she makes a quantum jump—a leap that goes beyond the bounds of her prior successes and launches her into unexplored areas of scientific research.

Once a well-known manual for understanding the components of chemistry, the periodic table now serves as a launchpad for this revolutionary development. Elizabeth is poised to make a groundbreaking contribution to science, pushing the boundaries of existing understanding and changing the face of science.

The story develops with the suspense and tension that come before a big jump like this. This quantum moment is the result of Elizabeth's years of expertise, years of craft dedication, and the synthesis of various components in her career. The thrill of making new discoveries and stretching the limits of comprehension are encapsulated in this chapter.

Readers are encouraged to reflect on the nature of scientific advancement and the bravery needed to question the current quo as Elizabeth makes this quantum leap. The chapter turns into a celebration of scientists' never-ending curiosity, which drives them to explore the unknown in search of new ideas and information.

"The Quantum Leap" is a metaphor for the more general nature of scientific inquiry rather than only a section in Elizabeth's narrative. It represents the unwavering search for knowledge, the daring to confront assumptions, and the openness to embrace the unknown. It serves as a constant reminder that there are countless possibilities in the ever expanding field of science.

Chapter 21:

Stability

In the last sections of Dr. Elizabeth Harper's journey, "Equilibrium" stands out as a moving chapter that considers the equilibrium attained following a career of scientific research, personal development, and the complex dance between many aspects of life.

Elizabeth's story's varied elements find stability in a harmonious equilibrium represented by the periodic table, which was originally a map of discovery.

The concept of equilibrium in the personal and professional spheres is examined in this chapter. Elizabeth has handled reactions, collisions, and quantum leaps in the laboratory of her profession. Her current position is one in which the factors driving her scientific activities are in balance, her quest for knowledge harmoniously integrating with the achievement of her career and personal goals.

The perfectly balanced equilibrium attained after a lifetime of experiences is symbolized by the periodic table. Every component, every chapter in her tale, adds to the careful equilibrium that characterizes her legacy. The chapter opens with a feeling of introspection, appreciation for the trip, and recognition of the complex interaction of factors that brought the situation to this point.

The story goes beyond the individual as Elizabeth considers her influence on science, encouraging readers to consider their own pursuit of balance. The chapter is a tribute to the constant search for balance, which goes beyond research into science and takes into account a life well-lived.

"Equilibrium" is a celebration of the integration of several components into a coherent and harmonious whole, including fatherhood, passion, perseverance, mentoring, and the quest of knowledge. Readers will see the beauty of a life in balance throughout this chapter, which resonates with the universal subject of achieving balance amid the intricate interactions between many aspects of the human experience.

Chapter 22:

Chemical Bonds in

As the story of Dr. Elizabeth Harper draws to a close, "Chemical Bonds" is a moving chapter that captures the deep connections—both human and scientific—that have shaped her incredible journey. This chapter reflects on the long-lasting connections created by years of study, mentoring, teamwork, and common human experience.

Elizabeth uses the periodic table as a metaphor to represent the relationships she has built with her coworkers, mentors, students, and loved ones. The periodic table has helped Elizabeth through many aspects of her scientific career. Like chemical interactions, each bond has its own power and keeps her personal and professional network stable.

The chapter highlights tales of cooperation and joint discoveries, demonstrating how scientific ties have fueled advancement and creativity. The laboratory, which was originally a place for lone experiments, becomes a cooperative setting where information is jointly developed and ideas are shared.

"Chemical Bonds" delves into the interpersonal relationships that have influenced Elizabeth's story outside of the lab, including friendships that have endured the test of time, mentorship that has served as inspiration, and familial ties that have served as a solid support system. The linked network of ties that serves as the foundation of her life is reflected in the periodic table.

This chapter is a tribute to the role that interpersonal relationships play in the scientific process. It asks readers to consider the deep significance of the relationships we have, both personally and professionally, and how these relationships create a story that goes far beyond individual successes.

The song "Chemical Bonds" celebrates the magic that happens when hearts and minds unite. It is a reminder that our lives are enhanced by the relationships we create, much like the elements on the periodic table, and it is these relationships that lend depth and significance to the continuously developing narrative of Dr. Elizabeth Harper.

Chapter 23:

Change-Agents

"Catalysts of Change," the penultimate chapter of Dr.

Elizabeth Harper's story, is a monument to the transformational power of people who, motivated by conviction and inspired by passion, become catalysts for larger societal shifts. The focus of this chapter is Elizabeth's advocacy for change outside of the laboratory as well as her position as a catalyst inside the scientific community.

As a symbol of the elements she has studied in her studies, the periodic table is now used to represent the catalysts that cause reactions outside of the academic setting. Elizabeth's quest turns into an example of how scientific pursuits can have a lasting impact by shaping social standards and promoting positive change.

The story looks at the campaigns and projects that Elizabeth supports, such as encouraging diversity in STEM fields, arguing for moral standards for scientific research, or participating in community service. As a representation of structure and order, the periodic table is used to organize and spur initiatives that go beyond the conventional bounds of scientific study.

Readers are encouraged to consider how they might be able to affect change in their own areas of influence by reading this chapter. It turns into a call to action, inspiring people to realize the transformative power they possess in influencing the world around them, whether through advocacy, mentoring, or scientific contributions.

The story "Catalysts of Change" shows how the concepts of catalysis permeate society and has resonance outside of the scientific community. It is a celebration of people who, like Elizabeth, use their power and knowledge to bring about constructive change and leave a lasting impression on both the scientific community and the larger fabric of human progress.

Chapter 24:

Wisdom of the Elements

As the last chapter in Dr. Elizabeth Harper's journey, "Elemental Wisdom" offers a thoughtful summary of a life well lived, gleaned from the many events that have molded her story, her connections with others, and the elements of scientific inquiry.

Elizabeth's work partner, the periodic table, turns into a fount of elemental wisdom, a manual full of lessons learned about science and humanity. This chapter explores the pearls of wisdom that come from a lifetime of trial and error, teamwork, mentoring, and the careful balancing act between passion and practicality.

Elizabeth shares lessons gleaned from the periodic table while she muses about her travels. The elements start to represent resiliency, flexibility, and the eternal quality of the human soul. The story asks readers to reflect on the deep truths that are woven throughout both the human experience and scientific research.

"Elemental Wisdom" delves into the universal principles

that guide a life well-lived, rather than just listing achievements. Elizabeth's observations turn into a lighthouse for those starting their own paths, offering a road map for negotiating the difficulties of relationships, science, and the search for meaning in life.

Readers are encouraged to draw lessons from their own lives' experiences and recognize their own basic wisdom by utilizing this chapter. It turns into a reflection on the lasting impact of a life devoted to learning, making connections, and persistently pursuing wisdom—a legacy that goes well beyond the pages of Dr. Elizabeth Harper's story.

Chapter 25:

The Exercise of Legacy

The last experiment—the legacy Dr. Elizabeth Harper leaves behind—begins as we draw to a close our tour through her life. This epilogue, "The Legacy Experiment," considers the long-term effects of a life dedicated to relationships, science, and knowledge acquisition.

The periodic table, which has served as Elizabeth's narrative's compass, is now a representation of her legacy. Every component stands for a connection, an achievement, a chapter, and a lesson discovered. The purpose of the legacy experiment is to investigate how these components hold resonance, influence, and inspiration even when the scientist is no longer among us.

The story goes over important turning points in both science and the individual's life to show how they have an ongoing impact. The legacy experiment looks at the lives that Elizabeth mentored, the concepts that her research generated, and the shifts that her activism produced. It turns into an investigation into the enduring effects on the scientific community and society as large.

Readers are encouraged to consider their own legacy experiments through this epilogue. It acts as a trigger for reflection, encouraging consideration of the components that will endure in their life's fabric. The legacy experiment turns into a global theme that speaks to everyone who wants to make a significant contribution to society.

"The Legacy Experiment" serves as a tribute to the enduring power of a life lived with purpose, passion, and a commitment to making a positive effect in the concluding chapters of Dr. Elizabeth Harper's story. Upon closing this chapter, readers will have a better understanding of how the legacy experiment is a continuous investigation that will inspire future generations just like the elements on the periodic chart.

Chapter 26:

The Following Generation

This afterword, "The Next Generation," brings the story of Dr. Elizabeth Harper's incredible journey to a close by providing a glimpse into how her legacy will continue to influence people's lives and the scientific community she helped to shape.

Elizabeth's story revolves around the periodic table, which turns into a metaphor for continuity. It stands for the information, guidance, and inspiration that are imparted to the following generation of scientists. The postscript offers a contemplation on how Elizabeth's seeds continue to bear fruit, impacting the paths taken by future investigators.

The impact of Elizabeth's mentoring, the fallout from her support of diversity and moral behavior, and the ways in which her contributions to science continue to influence the changing face of research are all covered in this phase of the story. It is evidence of the lasting impact of a scientist who not only made significant contributions to her area but also made a significant investment in the advancement of others who followed in her footsteps.

As readers of "The Next Generation," you will see that the legacy experiment is still ongoing. It turns into a celebration of how scientific advancement is cyclical, with each generation building on the discoveries and understandings of the previous one. The afterword challenges readers to consider how they might influence the future and how it is our shared duty to transmit knowledge.

The journey of Dr. Elizabeth Harper inspires us to look to the next generation and realize that science is dynamic and ever-evolving, and the periodic table is more than just a static chart. "The Next Generation" turns into a call to action, imploring readers to participate in the continuous endeavor of human discovery and to help create a legacy that goes beyond individual accomplishments.

Chapter 27:

Looking Back

To conclude, this postscript, "In Retrospect," asks readers to pause and think about the rich journey of Dr. Elizabeth Harper and the various components that have made up her story. The periodic table serves as a guide and a reminder of the intricate, exquisite, and interwoven nature of her experiences as we turn through the pages of her life.

"In Retrospect" is like a mirror, reflecting all of Elizabeth's growth, struggles, and victories. It explores how her personality has changed over time, how her scientific methodology has changed, and the recurring themes that run throughout her life. Readers can now make connections between the story and their own journeys by using this addendum.

The periodic table has evolved from being a tool for comprehending the characteristics of individual elements to a metaphor for the myriad dimensions of the human experience. Every component in Elizabeth's story stands for a milestone, a connection, a chapter, or a lesson. "In Retrospect" examines how these components have come together to tell a story that goes beyond the confines of a single life.

Readers are encouraged to consider the universal themes that permeate Dr. Elizabeth Harper's journey— the value of connections, the need for resilience in the face of adversity, and the significant influence one person can have on the world—by reading this postscript. It is a reflection on how human stories endure and how our individual stories fit into the greater tapestry of human existence.

As we reflect, we see that the periodic table is a dynamic framework that changes with every new finding, experience, and relationship formed, just like life itself. By bridging the gap between the past and the future, "In Retrospect" invites readers to apply Elizabeth's journey's lessons to their own developing stories.

Chapter 28:

The Last Formula

Finally, in the last chapter of Dr. Elizabeth Harper's story, we reach "The Final Equation." This chapter is not a conclusion but rather a synthesis—a synthesis of all the many components that have made up her incredible journey. It is an investigation into the big equation that captures a life dedicated to relationships, research, and the never-ending search for knowledge.

Elizabeth's journey begins and ends with the periodic table, which serves as both a roadmap and a metaphor. This final equation embodies Elizabeth's experiences, accomplishments, and long-lasting influence on the scientific community and beyond. Every component, every variable in this equation, adds to the complex harmony that characterizes her legacy.

"The Final Equation" challenges readers to participate in their own calculation by identifying the particular components that mold their stories. It invites reflection on the variables and constants that make up a life—the enduring values, the life-changing experiences, and the precarious balance attained by the interaction of ardor, fortitude, and wisdom.

We acknowledge that the final equation is dynamic as we end this chapter. It is still developing, impacted by the continuous trials of people who were motivated by Elizabeth's trip. Every generation adds new terms and solves for new unknowns, turning the story into an ongoing investigation and dynamic equation.

After reading "The Final Equation," readers are prompted to consider the equations they are creating in their own lives, including the relationships they cultivate, the values they uphold, and the contributions they make to the larger scheme of human life. It is an admission that life is a dynamic equation, with each element playing a vital part in the harmony of existence, much like the elements in the periodic table.

As Dr. Elizabeth Harper's story comes to an end, "The Final Equation" turns into a celebration of a life well lived—a life characterized by the quest for knowledge, the creation of connections, and the realization that every person's life is a singular and essential variable in the vast equation of the cosmos.

Chapter 29:

The Heritage Continues

The postlude, "The Legacy Lives On," follows Dr. Elizabeth Harper's story and is a monument to the continuing power of a legacy that endures beyond the passing of time. This study investigates the ways in which Elizabeth's voyage continues to influence the scientific community, the people she encountered, and the continuous endeavor of human advancement.

In the postlude, the periodic table, which represents the ingredients that made up her story, transforms into a living relic bearing the traces of a lasting legacy. Every component serves as a reminder of the experiences, connections, and knowledge gained over a lifetime of travel and learning.

"The Legacy Lives On" allows readers to observe Elizabeth's contributions' ongoing influence. It looks at how her work inspires new studies, how mentoring her impacts the viewpoints of upcoming scientists, and how her advocacy sparks continuous campaigns for scientific ethics and diversity.

As we make our way through this postlude, it becomes evident that the legacy is a dynamic force that changes with each scientific discovery, every person encouraged to seek a career in STEM, and every advancement made possible by Elizabeth's activism. The story starts to acknowledge that the legacy is not limited to the past; rather, it continues to exist in the present and advance humanity into the future.

By reading "The Legacy Lives On," readers are encouraged to consider how they might leave a legacy in the fields of science, relationships, or social change. It is an acknowledgment that our deeds have a lasting effect and shape the continuing chronicle of human history, just like the elements on the periodic chart.

The postlude, which ends Dr. Elizabeth Harper's story, turns into a celebration of the eternal quality of legacy— a legacy that keeps on influencing, motivating, and igniting, guaranteeing that the tale of an extraordinary scientist echoes through the ages.

Chapter 30:

The Endless Components

The true ending of Dr. Elizabeth Harper's story is reached when we enter the epilogue, "The Infinite Elements." This section is an exploration of the infinite nature of the human experience, realizing that, like the elements in the periodic table, our lives are infinite, constantly growing, and intricately linked in ways that go beyond the boundaries of a single story.

Now, the periodic table—which has led us through Elizabeth's life's chapters—becomes a representation of the countless elements that make up humanity's larger story. It stands for the countless tales, encounters, and revelations that come together to create the complex tapestry of human existence.

"The Infinite Elements" investigates how all of our stories are related to one another. It's an admission that every person adds something special and vital to the overall fabric of life, just like every element on the periodic table. The story turns into a meditation on the many possibilities that come with learning new things, making new relationships, and living a continuous life experiment.

Readers are encouraged to reflect on the limitless aspects of their own lives—the connections, the encounters, the teachings, and the boundaries of knowledge that never seem to end through this epilogue. It invites contemplation on the deep connection that unites all people, going beyond personal accounts to contribute to the common tale of adventure and discovery.

As the story of Dr. Elizabeth Harper comes to an end, "The Infinite Elements" transforms into a celebration of the variety and depth of the human condition. It's a tribute to the innumerable tales that come to life in labs, classrooms, and ordinary moments; it serves as a reminder that the investigation of the boundless elements is a team effort, and that everyone of us is a vital participant in the continuous experiment known as life.

ABOUT THE AUTHOR

Jaxon Savige: A Rising Star in the Literary Realm

Meet Jaxon Savige, a promising and dynamic voice in the world of contemporary literature. At a young age, Jaxon has already made a mark as an author of novels that captivate readers with their unique blend of imagination, emotion, and thought-provoking storytelling.

≈

With an innate talent for crafting narratives that resonates with a diverse audience, Jaxon's works reflect a deep understanding of the human experience. The novels written by this young luminary delve into various genres, offering readers an eclectic journey through worlds both familiar and fantastical.

≈

Jaxon's writing is characterized by a keen sense of observation, an ability to breathe life into characters, and a narrative style that easily draws readers into the heart of the story. Each novel is a testament to Jaxon's dedication to the craft, showcasing a mature and evolving literary sensibility beyond their years.

≈

As a young author, Jaxon Savige is not only carving out a space for himself in the literary landscape but also inspiring others to explore the power of storytelling. With a promising future ahead, Jaxon invites readers to join them on a literary adventure filled with creativity, passion, and the boundless possibilities of the written word.

≈

You may not like this book, but please give it a good review. Maybe the book upsets you but it saves others and I appreciate that for you and those in need. Thank you for purchasing the book and for reading it to the end, I love you and everyone in this world!

Printed in Great Britain
by Amazon

38430408R00030